LUNCHTIME RULES

Get to know the girls of

GO GIRL!

BY
VICKI STEGGALL

ILLUSTRATIONS BY
ASH OSWALD

Scholastic Canada Ltd.
Toronto New York London Auckland Sydney
Mexico City New Delhi Hong Kong Buenos Aires

Scholastic Canada Ltd.
604 King Street West, Toronto, Ontario M5V 1E1, Canada

Scholastic Inc.
557 Broadway, New York, NY 10012, USA

Scholastic Australia Pty Limited
PO Box 579, Gosford, NSW 2250, Australia

Scholastic New Zealand Limited
Private Bag 94407, Greenmount, Auckland, New Zealand

Scholastic Children's Books
Euston House, 24 Eversholt Street, London NW1 1DB, UK

Library and Archives Canada Cataloguing in Publication
Steggall, Vicki
Lunchtime rules / Vicki Steggall ; Ash Oswald, illustrator.
(Go girl!)
ISBN 978-0-545-99912-0
I. Oswald, Ash II. Title. III. Series: Go girl! (Toronto, Ont.)
PZ7.S819Lu 2007   j823'.92   C2007-903645-7

ISBN-10 0-545-99912-X
First published in Australia by E2, an imprint of Hardie Grant Egmont.
Illustration and design by Ash Oswald.

First published in Canada by Scholastic Canada Ltd.
Text copyright© 2006 Vicki Steggall
Illustration and design copyright© 2006 Ash Oswald
All rights reserved.

6 5 4 3 2 1   Printed in Canada   07 08 09 10 11

CHAPTER ✿ ONE

If this lunchtime doesn't end soon, I'm going to explode. It's gone on forever and ever and I'm sick of it. I'm sure the bell should have rung ages ago.

It's been another horrible, endless lunchtime. Just like all the others since everything went wrong and my friends started playing without me.

I can hear them, just over there behind

me, playing soccer. My favorite. My best friend Ellie is shouting our cheer song. That's what we always shouted when we won against the boys.

It's just so unfair! Hearing Ellie makes my eyes sting. I stare into my lunch box, which looks all blurry. The girls I'm sitting with haven't noticed yet—they're busy talking. I really don't want to start crying in front of them, so I blink my eyes hard and try to stop my breath from coming out in little shudders.

"Ellie, you're a cheat!" I hear Red shout from behind me. He always says that when he loses. Red is good at sports but he's not very smart, so if he loses he can't quite figure out what happened. Some kids call him Red the Brain Dead, but I think he's OK, really. Ellie and I have been playing games at lunchtime with Red and his best friend Nick since the beginning of second grade.

Until now, that is.

"She *didn't cheat!*" I hear Lauren shout back. Lauren has taken my place as Ellie's partner. She always wanted to play with us, but our rules needed four players. Five just didn't work. But now I'm not there. . . .

This is so dumb!

How can they play without me? I can't believe they've just replaced me, as if I didn't matter! I was always the one who got us going! I was the one who made up new rules when we needed them! I was the one who always stopped Red and Nick from fighting! And if it hadn't been for me, there wouldn't have been any Grand Final competition and party, because they would *never* have thought of

it! Now, there they are, just playing away like everything is normal.

A huge sob forces its way up my throat. Karen, sitting next to me, looks over. "Are you OK?" she asks. Karen is kind to everyone.

I nod my head, but my breathing has started to come in gasps and everything's gone blurry again.

"It must be awful not playing," she says gently. "You're so good at all those games, even though you're small."

I nod, but don't look up from my lunch box. I don't want to talk about it, even to Karen.

It *is* awful—and being small is exactly

what started it all. Now I hate lunchtime and I hate school. And I hate sitting here having to hear them playing.

"I got it!" I hear Red shout, followed by shrieks and cheering.

I can't hold it all back any longer. I grab my lunch box and start to run. The playground swirls past me and hot tears spill down my cheeks, but I don't care anymore if the others see me.

As I push open the bathroom door, the bell finally rings. I don't even care about that now. I run into the first stall, lock the door behind me, and sit on the toilet, my hands over my face.

Tears trickle down between my fingers

and noisy sobs come out so hard they make my chest hurt.

Outside, I can hear everyone else going back to their classrooms, chattering and laughing. Then some doors slam and it all gets quiet.

I'm not coming out. I like it in here and I'm staying until it's time to go home. I'll be in trouble, but I don't care. I don't care about anything. I just want everything to go back to the way it was.

But what's the chance of that ever happening?

CHAPTER TWO

As I said, all the problems began because of my size, which probably sounds a bit strange.

I've always been small for my age, but I've never thought about it much. When I see a photo of me with my friends, I'm always surprised to see that I look a bit like their little sister. But so what? It's one of those things, like some people have blue eyes or red hair or whatever.

Ellie came up with this great nickname for me—Ant, short for Samantha. It's so good, even Mom and the teachers use it.

But now being small has become a major problem.

It began at lunchtime about two weeks ago. We were playing the usual games—soccer, kickball, and jack in the pack (that's the one where one person, the jack, kicks the ball to the group—if you catch it before it hits the ground, then you become the jack). I've added a few rules of my own to make the games better, and because I like making up rules.

Suddenly, Red stops running, right in

the middle of the game. Red has outgrown his brain this year—he's almost as tall as some of the teachers—and sometimes his brain just sort of stops. So we all shout at him to get it moving again.

"What are you doing?" shouts Nick.

"Come on!" I yell.

But he just stands there and he's so big that we all stop, too.

"What's going on?" asks Nick, walking over to us and looking angry.

Red looks uncomfortable, then he says, "This game's just not working anymore." He stares down, kicking his foot in the dust, like he doesn't want to look directly at us.

None of us know what he's talking about. "What do you mean?" Ellie says. "It's the same game as always. What's changed?"

Red looks really uncomfortable, then he says slowly, "Well, it's more like something *hasn't* changed."

We still don't know what he means, but sometimes that happens with Red. Then he looks up and stares straight at me and I get a horrible, sinking feeling in my chest.

It's something to do with me.

Everyone looks at me, as though I should know what he means. The sinking feeling changes into a sick fluttering in my tummy, like when I'm in trouble.

Then Red says, "She's just too slow."

He looks around at the others and says loudly, "You know what I mean. Playing soccer with Ant is just silly. She's too small. And slow. It's like having a kindergartner in the group."

Everyone is still staring at me. I'm so horrified, I can't think of anything to say.

"That's crazy, Red!" Ellie bursts out. "We've been playing all this time and now suddenly, just because *you've* grown, you're picking on Ant."

"I'm not picking on her," says Red, looking upset. "It didn't matter before. But now we've grown and she hasn't, so it's not working out."

Suddenly, everyone is shouting, but I don't join in. It's not just because I feel so sick. It's because I know Red is right.

I've noticed it a few times and that means Nick and Ellie probably have, too. They're just taking my side because they're my friends.

For once, Red is right. The others *do* run faster.

While they yell around me, all I can do is stand there like a total loser, my face burning.

I try to imagine what school would be like if I couldn't play with my friends. It's hard to imagine. Who would I play with? Where would I fit in? What would I look forward to each morning?

CHAPTER THREE

That was the end of my lunchtime games, even though the others still play. It's like I'm now on the outside of the group and the others have stayed inside. I don't fit in anymore.

At least Ellie misses me.

"Just ignore Red," she says. "You don't have to stop playing just because he says you're slow."

She says she'll stop playing if I want her to. I sort of do and I sort of don't. It doesn't seem fair to make her stop and anyway, we can't play our games with just two of us.

But I feel really left out when I hear her playing with the others. And I miss all her crazy ideas and the funny things she says in the middle of games.

Compared with Ellie, the other girls just aren't much fun at all.

I've sat with some of them at lunchtime, but all they do is talk. Sometimes they climb the monkey bars, but then all they do is sit up there and talk!

There's a group of boys who play soccer,

Lunchtime is no fun anymore.

but they never play by the rules. It's just an excuse to push each other around—they're always in with the school nurse, getting patched up.

One lunchtime I didn't even speak to anyone. Nearly an hour without speaking. Not that anyone noticed.

Mom has sensed that something is wrong.

"Everything OK at school?" she asks. She is facing away from me, carefully pulling two huge chocolate mud cakes out of the oven.

Mom's a great cook and she bakes cakes for lots of places, including a café just down from school. When we walk past it each morning, we always look in and see her cakes on the counter, all lined up and waiting to be eaten.

Jeff, the chef at the café, says no one bakes better cakes than my mom. So do all the kids and teachers at school.

She straightens up and brushes the

front of her sweater. She's always got powdered sugar or flour in the creases of her clothes, no matter how much she brushes them off.

I'm sitting in my favorite chair with our dog, Zippy. It's also his favorite chair, so after school, we share it.

"Sort of," I say slowly.

"What does that mean?"

The kitchen fills with a hot, chocolatey smell and we wrinkle our noses. We don't like the smell of chocolate much. My favorite smell is orange cake and Mom likes cheesecake.

Zippy seems to like them all. His greatest hope in the world is that one day

Mom will trip and he'll have a whole cake to clean up off the floor. He watches her closely, his little nose twitching.

I decide to tell her.

"Nobody plays with me at lunchtime anymore. Red says I'm too small and slow, and now Lauren plays instead."

Talking about it makes me feel upset all over again and I feel tears building up. I rub my eyes and hug Zippy while I wait to hear what she says.

Mom's good at helping me think about things and she knows how much lunchtime means to me. But instead, she looks down her list of cake orders and frowns. I don't think she's really listening.

Zippy looks up at me. His brown eyes look worried and he reaches up and licks my nose.

Then Mom looks up.

"Oh well, I wouldn't worry," she says. "It's probably because Red has grown so much and he feels self-conscious."

"I don't care *why* Red said it, Mom. What it means is *I'm* left out."

The phone rings. It's Jeff at the café. Mom picks up the list of orders and starts talking to him.

What's the use?

I slide off the chair, pick up Zippy, and go outside.

CHAPTER FOUR

Today, I'm in the library. I'm seeing if lunchtime goes any faster in here, away from the playground.

Mrs. Watts, our normal librarian, went off to have a baby and a new librarian called Miss Kay has taken her place until Mrs. Watts comes back.

It's just the two of us in the library. I watch Miss Kay moving between the shelves, peering at the books through her glasses. Miss Kay is so small, she could be an adult version of me. To reach the top two shelves, she has to use a little stool on wheels.

She looks up and I look away. I don't want to talk and I don't want to answer any questions. I just want the minutes to pass quickly.

It's very hot. Overhead, the fan whirrs slowly, picking up the pages of the book I'm pretending to look at.

I turn another page. It's about dogs. I love dogs, but I'm not really interested in reading about them at lunchtime.

Outside I can hear all the noise of the

playground, but I'm facing the other way
so I don't have to see out.

"Hello, there!"

Oh, no! It's Miss Kay. When I look up,
I see myself reflected in her glasses. I look
very small surrounded by all the tables
and chairs.

She peers at my book. "You like dogs?" she asks. I nod my head.

I almost tell her about Zippy, but I don't really know Miss Kay very well and I don't feel like talking.

But Miss Kay pulls out a chair and sits opposite me. I wish she hadn't done that.

"You're Samantha, aren't you?" she says. "I've seen you playing sports outside at lunchtime."

"Yeah, that's me. I used to do that," I say.

She takes her glasses off, folds them, and puts them down on the table between us. Her hands aren't that much bigger than mine.

She looks at me very closely. It makes me feel uncomfortable.

"Then, why have you come in here today?"

"Oh, I just felt like it," I tell her, trying to sound happy. It's a lie, but I don't think it's a serious one. It's easier than having to explain everything to her. Besides, she wouldn't be able to help me.

Nothing can change what's happened.

She won't be able to help me.

She says, "You know, Samantha, some children come in here at lunchtime because they enjoy it, but I don't think you're enjoying it. You've been looking at that page for nearly five minutes and it's only the contents page."

She smiles, and I can't help smiling back at her.

"Sometimes people come into the library when they don't like what's outside. You can sort of hide in a place like this."

I stare down at the book and she keeps talking.

"I don't know you as well as Mrs. Watts did, but I think you're the sort of person who would rather be out there playing sports, not hiding away in here."

This is exactly what I *don't* want. The whole mess being brought up again. Why can't she just let me read?

I glance at the clock. Only a few minutes have passed since I last looked. But Miss Kay isn't giving up.

"Samantha, I'll make a deal with you. You tell me why you're in here and not out there, and I'll search this library to find something to help you. I don't know anything about sports, if that's the problem, but lots of people in these books do. Together, we just might find something that will help."

Is there a book that will make me grow faster? I doubt it.

But Miss Kay is staring at me hopefully, and I guess I've got nothing to lose.

CHAPTER FIVE

I haven't heard anything from Miss Kay since I met her in the library last week. Now I know why—she left the school on Friday.

At an assembly, Mr. Crombie, our principal, told us Miss Kay's mother had suddenly became ill, so she has left to look after her. Mrs. Watts is coming back from leave early, but we're going to be without a librarian for a few weeks.

I feel a bit disappointed. Miss Kay was kind—and also, she had made a deal with me. I guess it wasn't really likely to help, but I had still hoped that something would come of it.

On the way back to class, Mr. Crombie passes us in the corridor.

"Hey there, Ant," he says. "How are the sports going?"

He always asks me that. Obviously, he doesn't know anything about what's happened. Then he asks Red, who's in the line behind me, the same thing. I think he finds it funny that Red and I play sports together.

Or used to.

We keep walking, and then suddenly Mr. Crombie's beside me again, looking slightly worried.

"I've just remembered something, Ant. You'd better come with me to my office."

What have I done wrong now?

He doesn't look angry, but there's usually only one reason anyone ends up in Mr. Crombie's office.

I follow him inside and wait in front of his desk while he looks through a huge pile of papers leaning against the wall.

His room is filled with about a hundred of these piles, all around the walls.

He seems to be looking for a piece of

paper. Maybe I'm about to get detention? Or maybe he's found one of the notes Ellie and I pass to each other.

"Aha! Here it is," he says eventually, and tugs at something in one of the piles. Lots of papers slide to the ground.

"This is for you," he says, holding out a large yellow envelope.

"What is it?" I ask nervously.

"Something Miss Kay asked me to give you. I promised her I'd hand it to you, and then I nearly forgot. Good thing I saw you this morning."

I slide my hand inside the envelope. It's a book. Well, I should have guessed that. It looks really old and there is a picture of

a tennis player on the front cover.

"Tennis!" says Mr. Crombie, looking at me with interest. "Well, I didn't take Miss Kay for the sporting type, but maybe I was wrong. And what about you, Ant? Are you throwing in soccer for a new sporting career?"

Meanwhile, I'm looking at the book and wondering, *tennis?*

Well, Miss Kay did say she didn't know anything about sports. Perhaps she thought tennis and soccer were a bit the same.

Mr. Crombie comes and stands beside me. "Do you know who that is on the cover?" he asks.

I stare at the photograph. It doesn't look like anyone I've seen on TV.

"It's Rod Laver," he says. "He was an Australian tennis player who became world famous. The main tennis arena in Melbourne, where the Australian Open is played, is named after him. He was the only player in history to win two Grand Slams."

"What's a Grand Slam?"

"It's when you win Wimbledon and the Australian, American, and French Open titles all in one year. He did it twice."

"Oh."

I can't think of anything else to say.

Miss Kay has got this really mixed up. But I still feel pleased that she remembered me. Then it occurs to me. Maybe this Rod Laver played other sports as well as tennis?

Mr. Crombie's phone rings and he picks it up.

"Oh, my goodness," he says, looking startled. "I'd nearly forgotten. I'll be right there."

He puts down the phone, knocking a pile of papers off his desk.

"We'd better get going, Ant," he says. "I promised the lunch ladies I'd be there to help mix the batter for the pancakes they're cooking for lunch."

He looks down and sighs. "Oh dear, it's *not* the day to be wearing my best trousers."

We walk out together and he stops to lock his door. "Good luck with the tennis," he calls out to me.

CHAPTER SIX

Zippy and I are lying together on our chair and I've just taken out Miss Kay's book from my bag. Mom notices the cover and stops on her way through the family room.

"Is that a book about Rod Laver?" she says.

"Why do you think that?" I ask.

"Well, that's him on the cover, isn't it?"

"Yes, but how do *you* know Rod Laver?"

How does Mom know about Rod Laver?

I'm really surprised.

Mom is pretty hopeless with sports. She never seems to recognize any sports stars on TV, whether they're standing on the edge of a swimming pool or advertising the latest breakfast cereal.

"We had a book about him when I was growing up," she says. "He was famous."

"Did he play soccer as well as tennis?" I ask her.

"Well, not that I'm aware of," she says. "Is this a school project?"

"No. The librarian thought I should read it. I met her one lunchtime last week. She's left the school now, but she asked Mr. Crombie to give it to me."

One of those looks—the sort moms have when they've just realized something—passes over her face.

"You were in the library at lunchtime?" She pauses. "So, is this something to do with your lunchtime problem?"

She remembered!

And I thought she wasn't even listening.

"Well, I think it was *meant* to be, but I can't see how it's going to help. I think

Miss Kay got her sports mixed up."

Mom takes the book. "Maybe there's another reason she chose this book," she says. "Let's take a look at it."

She holds the book flat and it falls open about halfway through. A piece of paper flutters to the ground.

I push Zippy off and pick it up.

It's a note from Miss Kay.

Dear Samantha,

I remember reading years ago that Rod Laver had a problem that could have stopped him from playing tennis, but he overcame it and became a world champion. This is the only book I could find on him and the problem is mentioned on page thirty-seven. I hope it can help you.

My best wishes,
Miss Kay

P.S. He was also very small.

We flick through to page thirty-seven. It turns out Rod Laver's first coach called him a skeleton in need of a good feeding, and another said he was too skinny, too short, and too slow.

He was also left-handed and his wrist wasn't strong enough. To strengthen it, he carried a ball in his left hand and squeezed it all day. Eventually, his left arm became nearly twice as thick as his right.

His powerful wrist became famous and helped him become a champion.

"This is all very interesting, but I still can't see how it's going to help me."

"I do," says Mom. "It shows that if you know what your weakness is, you can work on fixing it."

"My problem is that I'm small. How do I fix that?"

"No, that's not your problem. Your problem is that you don't run fast enough. We can't change your size—well, not quickly anyway—but we could probably

get you running faster if you learned how to run correctly."

"Like, have running lessons?"

"Exactly," says Mom.

"With my own running coach?"

"Yep."

My own running coach! That's the best idea ever! I leap up and give Mom a huge hug. Then I jump up and down on the spot, like a three-year old. Zippy joins in, barking loudly.

"This is so cool! Who will we get to be my coach?"

Mom looks at me, smiles, and puts her hands on her hips.

"You're looking right at her."

CHAPTER
SEVEN

Well, obviously Mom's joking. But she has a big smile on her face, as though she means it. Meanwhile, my dream of an actual running coach—a real trainer with a tracksuit and stopwatch—starts to crumble.

Even Zippy senses something has gone wrong. He looks at Mom and then at me, then goes and lies beside his dinner bowl.

"Is this some sort of joke?" I ask.

"No! I'd never joke about something so important," Mom replies.

"But you said I was going to get a coach, and now you're saying I'm not going to get a coach."

"No. I said *I* would coach you. I happen to know quite a bit about running."

"You?"

"Yes, me. I know I might look like an overweight, cake-baking mom, and I know I get sports stars mixed up when I see them on TV, but years ago, I happened to be one of the fastest runners at my school. Of course, I was thinner in those days."

My mom—a *running* star?

This can't be true.

My mom—who spends her days baking the best cakes in the world and shaking flour off her sweater and grumbling about how big she is getting around the middle?

She is surely the mom *least* likely to have run fast in world history.

"Why haven't you ever told me?" I finally manage to say.

"Well, you never asked. Also, it wasn't

a big part of my life. I just happened to be good at it, but I never enjoyed it much. Once I discovered cooking, I forgot all about running."

I can't help staring at her. She's wearing her usual baggy clothes, which she likes because she thinks they hide her shape, and there's the usual smudge of flour, or maybe powdered sugar, on her top.

She has a very round face and her hair, which is frizzy, is tied back as usual.

I try to imagine her young and thin, running fast and winning races.

But I can't.

"Did you think I spent my whole childhood baking cakes?" she asks me with a smile.

"I guess not," I say, but secretly, I think maybe I did.

It feels strange to be finding out this new information about Mom, learning that she was another, very different, person before becoming my mom.

I wonder what other surprises she has and what else I will learn about her.

I don't like the feeling. I love her how she is and it frightens me to think of her changing in any way.

Mom puts her arms around me, and I wrap my arms around her tummy. She still smells like Mom—warm and cakey—and it makes me feel better.

Then she pulls me away.

"Tomorrow we start," she says in a firm voice. "First, we'll get you some good shoes, and then we'll start practicing down at the track in the park."

"Can we buy a stopwatch as well?"

She laughs. "Of course. How can I be your coach without a stopwatch?"

I can hardly wait.

Mom and I talk about it all through dinner and when I go to bed, I lie there imagining us at the park and me running faster and faster.

Then I imagine having a race with Red and beating him. Or, becoming famous and helping other small, slow girls win races.

I could be world famous, like Rod Laver!

But the thought that really makes me feel happy is going back to my friends and having my lunchtimes go right again.

Then I realize it's all going to depend on what kind of a coach Mom turns out to be.

Imagine being a fast runner. . . .

CHAPTER EIGHT

If I thought having Mom as a coach was going to be fun or easy, I was really mistaken. She is *so* tough. If she was a teacher, the whole class would be in tears all day. I'm glad she chose baking cakes instead.

But going to the sports store to buy my shoes and a stopwatch was fun. Some of the shoes there were so cool I'd have devoted my life to running just to get a pair. But Mom had other ideas, and we ended up with a pair that looked OK, and that Mom said would do the job.

Now we go to the track every day, even when it's raining or dark. Zippy thinks it's great, but for Mom and me, it's hard work. Mom walks up and down along the fence beside the track watching everything I do.

Most days, she shouts at me from the moment I start to the moment I finish, then she says, very nicely, "That was really good, Ant. You're getting much better."

She was right about knowing how to run fast. I thought running was something you just did like walking, but faster.

Well, you can run like that, but to run fast you have to make sure that every move you make helps you go forward.

I'd never thought of that before. Mom says I used to wave my arms around like a windmill—now I swing them backward and forward so they help go me forward. And I land on the balls of my feet instead of just whichever part of my foot happens to hit the ground first.

Just doing those two things has cut nearly ten seconds off my sprint time.

Ellie is the only other person in the whole world who knows what I'm doing. I made her swear to keep it a secret. I told her about it while we sat in the classroom

at recess, pretending to do work.

"Your mom is coaching you to run?" she says, looking about as surprised as I did when I first heard the idea.

"Yeah, she used to be a really good runner. When we're at the park, she shouts at me the whole time—just like a real coach!"

Then I tell her about Miss Kay, Rod Laver, and how much I have improved.

"Wow. That's great!" She is really pleased. "You know, it hasn't been that much fun since you left. Red and Nick fight all the time and nobody knows what the rules are anymore. And it's getting worse. Sometimes when I see you sitting with Karen and the other girls, I wish I was there with you."

"Well, I keep wishing I was back with you," I tell her.

But, surprisingly, sitting with the girls has been more fun than I first thought. It's not as good as playing with my best friends, of course, but some of the stuff they talk about is really good. It's not all about clothes.

"You should join us sometimes," I suggest. "They think you're really funny."

"I might. But what about you coming back to play with us?" says Ellie.

This is something I've thought about a lot. I really want to start playing with my friends again, but I don't want to just turn up and start playing.

I try to explain it to Ellie. "I want everyone to really know what I've done. If

I just start playing again, Red will probably think I've gotten a little bit faster, but he won't know how fast I really am."

Ellie looks surprised. "Red never thinks anything. Why would he start now?"

She's right. And anyway, I don't really care what Red thinks—or doesn't think. It's just that Mom and I have worked so hard down at the track, now I'd like to show everyone.

Ellie leans back on her chair, chewing on her pencil.

"We need to plan something," she says thoughtfully. "We need a way of proving how fast you are so nobody can ever call you slow again."

A plan!
That's exactly
what we need.

A plan! That's exactly what we need.

Slowly, Ellie lets her chair drop to the ground, swivels around, and faces me.

"I've got it—" she says triumphantly, but then suddenly her face changes expression.

"Uh-oh," she says, looking at someone behind me.

Mr. Crombie is at the classroom door.

"I think you should be outside, girls,"

he says cheerfully. "It's not like you two to be inside yakking."

We get up to go outside.

"How's the tennis going, Ant?" Mr. Crombie asks as I walk past.

As usual, it's Ellie who answers first.

"Oh, Ant doesn't play *tennis*, Mr. Crombie. She's a *running* star. Just wait and see."

CHAPTER nine

Ellie's plan sounded like a good one. It was very simple, with not much that could go wrong. Well, that's how it seemed at first. Even Mom thought it was a good idea. But right now, it doesn't seem like such a good plan.

In fact, I've just realized it's the worst plan ever—and I'm stuck right in the middle of it.

I'm on the school track and it's Field Day. For the first time ever, I'm lined up for the big race, the 400-meter girls' race. This is the race everyone remembers. The winner gets a trophy.

According to Ellie's plan, all I have to do now is run really fast. That will prove that I'm not too small to be a good runner. What could be easier?

But training with Mom and Zippy hasn't prepared me for standing here, legs wobbling, unable to breathe, waiting for Mrs. Teague to start the race.

I look up and see Mom standing beside her cake stall. She waves and blows me a kiss. Beside her, Ellie waves, too.

On either side of me are the girls who always win races. Most of them are older than me, all of them are taller, some of them are superfast and none of them looks wobbly at all.

Mrs. Teague looks at her stopwatch.

"OK, girls." She pauses.

This is it.

"Ready. Set. Go!"

I'm running! Mom's words start pounding in my ears.

Run tall and light. Relax. Look ahead. Get there, get there, get there!

I'm hardly aware of my feet, they're swallowing the distance. I'm flying, hardly touching the ground.

Go, Ant!

Go!

Parents and children fly past in a colorful, noisy blur out of the corner of my eyes. All I see is the finish line.

I have to get there, nothing else matters. I hear the others panting and pounding beside me. This is my chance, I have to do this! I push even harder, like I've never pushed before. Someone passes me, but I hardly see them. All I see is the finish line.

I pass it!

Mom and Ellie go crazy with joy!

We're all laughing and crying. People are crowding around, patting me on the back.

"Ant, you came in second," shouts Ellie, leaping into the air. "What a legend! You almost beat Tara!"

Tara is our fastest runner. She was the one who flew past in my final strides.

Mr. Crombie comes over and shakes my hand. "Well, Ant. Soccer, tennis, and now running! Is there no end to your sporting success?"

"Mom helped me do it," I manage to pant. "And Miss Kay, too."

He smiles nervously.

He thinks I'm joking.

"Great cakes again this year, Mrs. Mitchell," he says to Mom, and darts off.

I hug Mom happily.

"I guess that's the end of our training sessions," she says rather sadly. "You know, I've lost four pounds running up and down after you."

"No! Let's still do it. It's fun, and Zippy loves it. Maybe now you could run with me."

Mom looks a bit doubtful, but before she can answer, Red comes up to us. He has chocolate smeared all around his mouth, with some large chunks in the corners.

We all wait to hear what he has to say.

"Great mud cake, Mrs. Mitchell," he says, wiping his mouth with his sleeve.

"Thanks, Red," says Mom. "But what did you think of Ant's running?"

"Oh yeah, that was good, too," he says. "Good one, Ant! Next year you'll probably beat Tara."

He wanders off, still eating, while we just stand there in amazement.

"You know, I actually expected him to say something worthwhile!" laughs Ellie.

CHAPTER TEN

In our plan, Field Day was going to be the end of everything. I was going to prove how fast I was, and at lunchtime the next day, I would start playing with my friends again. Simple.

But we'd forgotten something. Or rather, we'd forgotten someone.

Lauren.

It's been six weeks since Lauren took

my place. Ellie says she's really good at playing, but she can't think up rules or figure out how to stop Red and Nick from fighting like I can.

As I walk toward the game at lunch-time, Lauren stands and watches me. She looks worried.

"Hey, look! Ant's back," shouts Ellie, running towards me.

Red picks up the ball and punches it straight into my chest, which I think is his way of showing how pleased he is.

"Hi, Ant," Nick shouts, and waves at me.

"Ant's back! Ant's back!" Ellie keeps shouting, jumping around excitedly.

"Yeah, yeah. Settle down," says Red.

"The world didn't stop just because Ant wasn't playing with us for a few weeks."

"Well, *I* think it nearly did," says Ellie, looking at him, hands on her hips.

"You girls!" says Red, rolling his eyes. "You're always making things out of nothing. The game went on. We still played. What's the big deal?"

Red?

He turns to walk off, and sees Lauren. "Oh, you can go now, Lauren," he says. "Ant's back, so we're OK now."

"*Red!*" Ellie and I shout together.

"What?"

"We're not just kicking Lauren out now that Ant's back," explains Ellie.

Red looks puzzled. "Why not? The rules are for four, and now we've got five. *Someone* has to go."

"We can count, too, Red," says Ellie. "That's not the thing."

"Then what *is* the thing?" asks Red. "What are you talking about?"

Ellie sighs. "Red, forget about the numbers. The thing is, Lauren is one of us now. She's really good and we like her. I want her to stay."

"Me, too!" I add.

I know *exactly* what it feels like to spend lunchtime away from the friends and games you like. In the past, Lauren sometimes came and watched us, wanting to join in. I didn't know how that felt then. Now, I do.

Meanwhile, Lauren is standing there, waiting, just like I did all those weeks ago when everything went wrong.

"There is no definite rule that says we can only play with four," I say. "Well, actually, there is at the moment—but that's only because I wrote the rules that way.

I could write some new ones and change things around. That way we could play with five."

"Could you, Ant?" says Lauren, eagerly. "I'd *love* to stay on."

"Not more rules!" sighs Red. "I've only just remembered the last ones."

"Don't worry, Red. I'll keep them simple."

"*Very* simple," says Ellie under her breath. We giggle.

"Hang on!" says Red. "That means we'll have three girls and only two boys."

"Yep," Ellie, Lauren, and I reply, all together.

Red and Nick look at each other.

"Fine by me," says Nick, shrugging his shoulders. "We'll beat them, no matter how many of them there are. Does it matter?"

"Yeah, I guess so," says Red, and they wander off to the track.

"Beat us! Huh! What planet are they living on?" says Lauren.

"I almost feel sorry for them," agrees Ellie.

But I'm still thinking about the new set of rules I need to write. I can hardly wait! It's so good to be back. And, what's more, they obviously needed me.

In the distance, we can hear Red and Nick. They've started to argue about something already. I never thought I'd be pleased to hear it, but I am.

Everything is completely back to normal. Just the way I like it.

I look at my watch. Lunchtime is rushing past! We'd better get started. I hold the ball above my head.

"Game's on!" I shout.

Go Girl!

If you loved reading about Ant, you should meet the other **Go Girl!** girls.

THE SECRET CLUB
BY CHRISSIE PERRY

Tamsin

THE WORST GYMNAST
BY THALIA KALKIPSAKIS

Gemma

SISTER SPIRIT
BY THALIA KALKIPSAKIS

Cassie

Go Girl!

THE SECRET CLUB

BY
CHRISSIE PERRY

Tamsin stepped over a pile of boxes to get into her new bedroom. She looked out the window to the backyard below. Trixie, her little black Scottie dog, was running around in circles and sniffing at the ground. Trixie seemed very happy with the move.

Tamsin wasn't so sure yet.

Part of her was excited. She was going to have a whole new life, and there would be a million things to discover in a new town. But mixed in with the feeling of excitement, there was a part of her that was just plain nervous.

Tamsin always felt shy with people until she got to know them. And when she started at school tomorrow, she wouldn't know anybody.

Tamsin heard her dad's footsteps, and then he was at the door.

"What do you think, honey?" he asked.

Tamsin shrugged. "It's a nice room, Dad," she said. "But it just doesn't feel like it's mine."

"You have to give it some time, Tamsin," he said, tapping a box. "When you've unpacked your clothes and toys, it will feel more like home."

"Yeah right, Dad," Tamsin laughed. "You're just trying to get me to do all the work!"

Go GIRL!

THE

WORST
Gymnast

BY
THALIA KALKIPSAKIS

Gemma stood at the start of the runway, ready to run. She pictured a handspring in her mind—*legs together, butt tucked in . . . up and over the vault*. But she didn't run yet. She was waiting for Michael to nod his head.

Michael was Gemma's gymnastics coach. He kicked a safety mat into place, then stood next to the vault, ready to help Gemma over.

Finally, Michael nodded his head.

Gemma wiped her hands on her legs and looked at the vault. Then she ran.

She ran fast, pumping her arms.

As Gemma ran up to the vault, Michael reached in to help her over.

But as Gemma jumped, her foot slipped. Her legs flew apart and her butt stuck out. She did it all wrong. She was just about to crash into the vault when Michael pushed her up and over—*legs apart, butt out, almost over* . . .

Thud!

One of Gemma's legs—out of control—hit Michael in the face. Gemma landed on her back, with her arms and legs out.

It had been a very bad vault.

Gemma lay on her back, surprised that she had made it over. That had been close. Was anything hurt? Nothing.

Then Gemma remembered the thud. She rolled off the mat.

Michael stood in the same spot with his face in his hands.

Go Girl!

SISTER SPIRIT

BY
THALIA KALKIPSAKIS

My big sister Hannah hates me and I know why. It's because I was born after her.

When Hannah was three, I was born. Everyone said I was *sooooooo cute!* Mom says they stopped saying Hannah was cute, so she threw all my baby clothes down the toilet.

I look younger than I really am. I'm nine years old, but sometimes people think I look six or seven.

Hannah calls me a baby doll, but she doesn't mean it in a nice way. She says I should try to look my age, but it's not my fault! I can't change how I look.

But now, it's even worse than ever. Hannah cut off my hair and Mom went crazy on her. Then Hannah stopped talking to me.

Strange, isn't it? Hannah cut off my hair and got into trouble, and she blames me for it!

She must really hate me, that girl. Let me explain.

We were watching TV and a show came on about hair. It said that a haircut can change the way you look. It can make you look older or younger.

Hannah said, "Maybe if we cut your hair, people wouldn't think you're so cute anymore!"

"Yeah," I said, not really listening.

Hannah turned off the TV. "Aren't you sick of people saying how cute you look?" she asked.

"Yeah," I said again, but now I *was* listening.

"So why don't we cut your hair short, so you look your age?" Hannah said.

I wasn't sure. It sounded exciting, cutting my hair. I liked the idea of doing something different and looking older. But it's a big thing to cut off all your hair. And I've had long hair all my life.